INFESTATION

DEANNA YOUNG

THE BROTHERS UBER

For my children—Trevor my starry eyed dreamer, Logan who never ceases to surprise me with his cleverness, Riley my sweet perfectionist, and Katelyn my sunshine. They are the reason for everything I do, and the reason I get next to nothing done. And for my husband. He has always supported and encouraged me as I chase my crazy dreams, even when he doesn't understand them. I love them more than all the words I've ever written could express.

CHAPTER 1

CIENA SEALED her helmet in place and opened the Hespres II's space station hatch. She triple checked the tether line, clipped her equipment to her suit, took a deep breath, and stepped out into the black abyss of space.

Getting rid of a ship's Rogue Autonomous Trasher problem wasn't hard, not anymore, but the hull inspection made her stomach tie in knots every time. She always saved this step for last.

Ciena pressed the controls that steered her suit, gliding toward the docked ship.

The O2 regulator sputtered, and her heart skipped a beat. She rapidly depressed the button as sweat beads formed on her forehead. Within seconds the propulsion system engaged, thrusting her forward and allowing her to angle back toward her target. She let out a shaky breath. She'd almost died in space once before, floating alone in a malfunctioning evacuation pod. Even with the security tether, she never felt safe outside the station.

Ciena reached for the guide rail that ran along the length of the ship and clipped herself onto it. The artificial gravity from the ship extended through the hull enough to pull her toward it, now that she was closer. She oriented herself, unhooked the large box attached to her pack and secured it to the rail beside her. Both the box and the slender, silver cylinder attached to it were her creations. The pipe called out to the RATs, sending subsonic signals that mimicked impacts against ships and distress beacons to attract RATs in the immediate area, and the box trapped them.

She pushed a button, activating her siren's pipe and opened the slot in the side of her modified Faraday trap.

The engineering involved in making the Trashers fascinated her. Originally designed to salvage old ships and tear down space junk, they were sturdy, nimble and efficient. Not necessarily a good quality when they went rogue, but it was a manageable problem. And it gave her a job.

Any second now. Yep. Here they come. Several squat robots with metallic legs made their way toward her. The RATs were roughly the size of a human hand, and looked more like crabs than rodents, but the acronym did fit with their infestation-like qualities.

One of the RATs floated toward the trap, carrying a metal scrap in a clawed hand, reluctant to abandon its find as it was pulled in by the siren's song. She opened a slot on the top of her trap and shoved it inside along with three others as they reached her.

She checked her scanners for any unusual movement in the area. There was always a straggler or two. Sure enough, a RAT scuttled toward her from the front of the ship using its magnetic limbs to grip the metal hull. It made it to the trap at the same time another RAT swept down from behind Ciena, making her rock back in surprise as it landed on the trap. She pushed it and its buddy into the trap with the others.

Confident now that they were all collected, she closed the slot door and activated a specialized EMP, frying their main fuses.

Ciena finished up by inspecting the ship and entering repair requests on the displayed holographic schematics. After two passes, she lit up the digital display inside her helmet to check the time and gasped. It was nearly noon. She had to hurry, or she'd be late for her chat with Abby.

The tether retracted, pulling her into the city-sized space station. She huffed at the slow and steady pace. There was nothing to be done about the speed, so she tried to relax and enjoy the view. This was something people traveled out of their way to see, and she was lucky enough to look out on it every day.

Tulorian, the planet the station orbited, was alive with violent storms, seemingly eager to perform for her. Deep purple clouds swirled and tumbled over each other, while blue lightning intermittently lit the planet's violet surface. This mesmerizing display was an extra incentive for travelers to stay a little longer at the resort station.

As the view diminished behind the looming station, Ciena glanced at the clock again. She still had time, but not much.

The hatch opened, pulling her in. It closed behind her, and the heavy artificial gravity locked her to the ground, momentarily jarring her senses. She shed her suit, not bothering to wait for the dizziness to subside, then picked up her RAT trap and started for the door. She could collect payment later.

A tall, thin man called out, chasing after her. "Miss! Are you done then? Can I get my writ of decontamination? I need to get on with my repairs."

She stopped and let out an exasperated sigh before composing herself and turning around, "Yes, of course." She waved the man forward. "I'll need payment before I sign the forms."

He dropped several blue spherical glass chips into Ciena's open palm. The small marble-like currency stuck together in a clump in her hand. Ciena raised an eyebrow at him and cleared her throat.

"What's this? The cost is fifty."

He bristled and looked down his nose as he spoke. "Yes, but I don't owe you for a full day of work. You did the job in just a few hours."

Ciena mimicked his condescending tone, "Yes, but you would have paid twice that if I had taken the standard two days. And you'd be waiting another day to start your repairs."

It had taken Ciena quite a while to get used to bargaining this way. No one ever wanted to pay her what her services were worth. Part of it was typical haggling, and part of it was that she was a nineteen-year-old girl, and looked like an easy mark. Ciena had spent nearly a year modifying her trap and building her pipe to make the job more efficient. But that didn't stop people from trying to convince her that she was ripping them off.

She kept her palm open, waiting. "You knew the price before I started."

The muscles in the waifish man's jaw tightened and he begrudgingly dropped one more chip in her still open hand. This chip was clear and the encased metallic bar in the center glinted as it tumbled against the other spheres and clicked into place at the bottom of the pile.

"Most generous. Thank you, chief," she said, pocketing the clicks and giving him a mock salute with two fingers.

He didn't respond, but held out his decontamination order instead.

She signed the proffered tablet, grabbed her RAT trap, and rushed out the bay doors.

After dropping the metal box and extra money off in her quarters, Ciena strode to the transport terminal, weaving her way through the meandering crowd. She hopped on the tram while those around her shuffled through the open doors, staggering into comfortable positions.

The sharp smell of hydraulic fluid filled the confined space, coming from a group of machine workers standing at the front of the car. Ciena dropped her cheek to her shoulder and discreetly sniffed the collar of her own jacket then relaxed against the wall behind her. Thank goodness those spacesuits were well ventilated.

They rode in consensual silence as passengers checked and stowed various devices from their pockets. Ciena shifted her weight from foot to foot, suppressing a sigh as the tram stopped to let more people on.

After getting a few strange looks, she realized she was still sporting her messy mane of helmet hair and fished a handful of ribbons out of her pocket. Her fingers eventually tamed the beast, weaving ribbons through the braids as she went.

Eventually the tram came to its final stop, spilling passengers out into the station's enormous common room.

She pushed past the newcomers gawking at Tulorian and the ongoing storm visible through the massive viewing windows and picked her way through the crowds of people milling in front of the various food establishments. She climbed the stairs leading to the balcony two at a time and walked briskly past men and women peddling services and goods from storefronts and kiosks, nodding to a few as she dashed past.

Inside the dull, sterile communications alcove of the relay station were dozens of cubicles, each with its own chair and large computer screen.

Ciena sat at one of the terminals and took twenty-five clicks out of her pocket. The little glass spheres stuck together in a clump. She pushed them apart with her thumb and let them click back together as she counted them. It wasn't much, the cost of a few nice meals and a hot shower, but she always felt a little sick when she had to spend money.

A soft chime sounded as she dropped the clicks one by one into the slot by the screen. It came to life, showing twenty-five credits. The haptic feedback of the keystrokes bounced around the empty room as she tapped out her chat request: 'Abby Holwick, Bitera Orphanage, Ophelia'.

While she waited for someone dozens of light years away to fetch Abby, Ciena pulled a bar of Survival Sustenance out of her pocket and tried to enjoy the chewy meal. She could have bought lunch while downstairs, but she purposely didn't bring any extra clicks with her so she wouldn't be tempted. While digging at the pits in her teeth with her tongue, trying to clear out pieces of the sticky goo caught there, she opened another window on the screen and checked the station logs. Three ships, including a full-sized cargo ship, were scheduled to dock later today, but only two had traveled through a sector that required decontamination. Regardless, she had a busy afternoon ahead of her. Tomorrow's roster was clear for now. If it stayed that way, she would have plenty of time to get caught up with her other work.

The meter in the top right corner of the screen now read '20 credits.' Ciena slouched forward in her chair, resting her elbow on her knee and propping her head on her hand. *Hurry, Abby.* She sighed and tapped the icon that said 'Book Travel.' An alphabetic listing of destinations came up, and she scrolled until she came to Ophelia. She tapped on it, and a picture of a watery planet with thousands of islands filled the screen. Two price tags lit the bottom left corner.

'Direct passage, all expenses paid, 36 days: 39,899 clicks'

'Passage via Ridel and Titan, basic accommodations, 72 days: 24,499 clicks'

Ciena opened another window and pulled up her station account. She had saved 34,743 clicks in a little over 2 years. She had more than enough to get to Ophelia already, but she wanted to be sure she wouldn't be stranded once she got there. If all went well, she could book passage for Ophelia in about a month. Hopefully, the extra money she had saved would not only be enough to get Abby, but also help them find someplace they could call home again.

Beep, Beeeeeeep.

An incoming message interrupted her thoughts. The picture of Ophelia was replaced by the face of a seven-year-old girl with wavy brown hair cut short above her ears. She was wearing a tan smock and sweat dripped down her face, making clean pink streaks in the brown dirt.

"Hi, Ciena," she said, lisping slightly through her semi-toothless grin.

Ciena's heart soared and ached all at once looking at her sister. "Hi, sweetie. How have you been?"

The screen froze, and for a few seconds Ciena worried that a solar flare might have cut off the communication. Before she could toggle away to reboot and resend, the delayed relay caught up in time for Abby's response. "I'm good. I did get in a tiny bit of trouble for making sand castles today when I was supposed to be planting." She looked sheepish for a second, then rushed on, "But I already finished with my barrel, and they never told me I had to help the others when I was done. I should have known better. It takes a lot of food to feed all of us and we have to do our part." She said the last part like a recitation.

"Well, I guess–" Ciena stopped, struggling to find the right response.

"Oh, and Pedra says to remind you to call *after* 6, Ophelia time. I still had fifteen minutes to plant."

Ciena couldn't help letting out a snort. They had changed approved call times twice in the last month alone. The last time the window they gave her didn't correspond with relay station alignment and Ciena had to miss the call. "Okay. I'll remember to call after 6."

Abby didn't need to see her upset, so she swallowed her frustration, and leaned toward the screen. "Guess what? I have some great news."

"What is it?" Abby asked with wide eyes.

"In about a month, I'll be heading your way. It'll still take a few months to get to Ophelia, but you can start counting down now. And, I'll make a hundred sand castles with you when I get there, okay?"

Abby let out a tiny squeal. "I can't believe you're finally coming."

Something off-screen drew Abby's attention, and she turned to look behind her.

Ciena gasped. A large, deep purple bruise ringed in red stood out on the back of Abby's arm.

"What happened to your arm?"

"Oh, it's nothing." She covered her arm with her other hand and rubbed it. Seeing Ciena's sharp look, she mumbled, "Just sat in the wrong spot at lunch. Some other kids didn't like it."

"Oh, Abby, I'm so sorry. Are they still being a problem?"

Abby shrugged and stared at the ground. "Pedra says that I shouldn't taunt them. But I wasn't. It's just, the other seats were full, and we aren't supposed to sit on the floor. It was stupid. I don't really want to talk about it. Okay?"

Ciena pursed her lips but didn't press the issue further. What had happened to the bubbly little girl who bounced when she walked because she couldn't contain her happy energy? The Abby she used to know was slowly disappearing. She'd have to write to Pedra later, not that it would do any good, but she had to try.

Ciena blinked to keep the tears at bay. Now was not the time to break down. "I'll be booking the next ship that comes through. It's scheduled to dock here in thirty-six days." By then, it would be almost two and a half years since they'd been in the same room together. Two and a half years since they were split apart by the event that shattered their world.

"Hey, you're wearing the ribbons momma gave you again. They look nice. I can't wear ribbons here." Abby said, brushing back the short hair that barely touched her ears.

Ciena absently touched the colored ribbons she had laced through her braids. Her mother had always loved braiding them in like that. She said it was like weaving a little bit of hope and happiness into her before sending her off to school. It was this kind of mom-magic that got Ciena through primary school. She wished she could do the same for Abby.

"Which color do you like best?" Ciena asked, tilting her head so Abby could see them better.

"Purple!" she shouted, then clapped a hand over her mouth and looked over her shoulder again. "I mean, purple is my favorite color. I love purple," she said more softly, ducking her head into her shoulders.

A hand landed on Ciena's shoulder, giving her a start.

She turned and looked up at a young man with short black hair and a wide grin.

"Hey, Ciena. Sorry to interrupt," he said. "My father…er, I mean, Commander Hamelin wants to speak to you."

A digitalized voice from the terminal broke in, *"Deposit more currency for additional minutes."*

"Um, just a second, Kienn," Ciena said, holding up one finger and turning around.

"Don't go yet." Abby's voice was almost too soft to hear. "It's almost dinner. Just talk a little bit longer. Please, so I don't have to go back out." She bit her lip and stared unblinkingly at Ciena through the screen.

"Thirty seconds remaining," the computer announced.

"Abby, I didn't bring any more clicks. I'm sorry." She leaned in closer and brought her hand up to touch Abby's digitalized face. Tears filled the little girl's amber eyes and her bottom lip trembled.

The deposit chime sounded, and Ciena turned to see Kienn dropping clicks into the circular slot.

He gave her a small shrug and whispered, "I'll wait for you outside." Then waved to Abby before turning and walking out the door.

———

Several minutes later, Ciena stepped out of the communications relay. Kienn jogged forward from where he had been leaning against the wall to join her.

She turned away and wiped her nose with her sleeve. "Sorry. It's just hard to see her like that. I'll pay you back later."

"Don't worry about it. Seriously."

Ciena rolled her eyes. "I *will* pay you back."

"Fine, fine." He raised his hands in mock surrender. "What was that all about, anyway? With your sister, I mean. Isn't she at the Home for Children on Ophelia?"

"Yes, if you can call it a home. They have those kids working in the fields or workshops all day. They say it teaches them valuable skills for the real world, but it's just free labor."

"I'm sorry. I didn't know it was that bad. I thought she was doing well there, that it was better for her."

"That's what everyone thought. It's not your fault. Nothing to be sorry about."

He looked down at his feet and didn't say anything while they walked past the Antique Arcade and descended the stairs. The pings and zings from the arcade faded as they left it behind.

The common room was bustling with activity. Kids giggled and ran around their parents as they haggled over the price of supplies, meals, or trinkets. Men and women alike laughed as they played cards and told stories, passing the time over drinks until their ship repairs were complete and they could hit the skies again.

A tall, thick man with crew-cut hair and a bushy beard walked up to the door in the engineering column at the center of the room. He stepped back and examined it, putting his hand on the keypad.

What is he doing?

Kienn seemed to be thinking the same thing and changed course to intercept him, "Can I help you?"

"Oh, yes. I'm looking for the gear smith. I need to rent a spatial aligner." His voice was low, his accent abrasive. Ciena couldn't see his face very well from where she stood, but his voice seemed strangely familiar. A feeling of distrust settled over her.

"The office is right next to Tram B, over that way." Kienn pointed behind the man.

He grunted his thanks and turned to head the direction Kienn indicated. As he spun, his left leg twisted at an odd angle. "Katha!" he swore under his breath, and limped away.

A chill fell from the base of Ciena's skull and scurried down her spine. The last time she'd heard that curse was the last time she ever saw her parents.

CHAPTER 2

CIENA STOOD FROZEN IN PLACE, staring at the man as he disappeared around the column. She fought the urge to follow and get a closer look at his face. Paranoia had caused her problems in the past. This part of the galaxy was full of Katalians; hearing bits of their language wasn't completely unusual. Still, she made a mental note to mention it to Commander Hamelin. Maybe it was nothing, but maybe not. She took a deep breath, willing her mind to stop thinking about it.

"Ciena? Are you coming?" Kienn asked.

"Yes." She brought her gaze back to where he stood. "Do you know why your father wanted me?" As a freelance employee, she rarely had reason to interact with the station commander.

Kienn pursed his lips into a thin line. "You know he doesn't talk to me about official business."

"So, it's official business then, huh? Did someone complain about my amazing efficiency again?"

He laughed and shook his head.

"Did someone say they found a stray RAT I missed, or something?" When she first started this gig, that was a common grievance. There are a lot of places on a ship that a fist-sized robot can hide. After months of trial and error, she found a solution through the invention of her siren pipe and RAT trap. No valid complaint had been filed since, so that couldn't be the problem. "Oh. I wonder if it was that skeevy guy from earlier. Did he complain that I made him pay the full amount?"

"I don't know. Maybe?" He shrugged.

She squinted at him, trying to tell if he was hiding something. He was never supposed to know any official business, but you could usually count on Kienn to know everything that was going on in the station, official or not. She couldn't afford any fines or suspensions right now. Not when she'd already promised Abby she'd be leaving soon.

"What?" He noticed her intense stare and nudged her with his shoulder, making her canter to the side a few steps. "I actually volunteered to come get you because I wanted to invite you to play some airball later. We haven't done anything together in a while." He ran a hand through his hair, smoothing down some of the dark waves. "My treat, of course. I need to redeem myself after that last game. I think my hover-pad was damaged or something."

She raised an eyebrow at him. "Damaged? The hover-pad was not damaged. Not sure about its rider, though." She punched him softly in the shoulder, glad to have something to take her mind off Abby and the commander.

He crossed his arms and turned to face her as they stopped in front of the office doors. "You only beat me by five points, and that hover-pad *was* acting up."

"Well, I'd be happy to give you a rematch then. It'll probably be after nine, or possibly tomorrow, though. I've got a pretty busy day ahead of me."

"That's perfect. I have to leave for a water mining run in just a bit. We won't be back until close to nine anyway. I'll send you a comm when I get back."

"Didn't you guys go just last week?" She tried to keep her voice casual, not whiney. When Kienn was gone, the station felt so empty.

"Yeah, but we've had several cargo fleets this week that needed their tanks refilled, so we're running low again." He shrugged and smiled in a *this is just station life* kind of way, then inclined his head toward the door. "Well, good luck. I'll see you after nine. And no messing with my hover-pad if you get there first." He wagged a warning finger at her as he walked backward, then turned and jogged off to the tram terminals.

"I've never done that!" she yelled after him.

Once his figure faded into the crowd, she turned back to face the office doors. She took a deep breath and pushed the entry button on the panel.

The doors opened with a low hiss and Commander Hamelin looked up from where he was standing, leaning over his desk. His thick eyebrows and short beard flecked with gray gave him an intimidating presence. Luckily for her, he didn't seem to be channeling that superpower at the moment. Instead he waved her in with a smile, which she took to mean she likely hadn't done anything wrong. Most of the rest of the tension melted away as she thought about how his family had taken her in and helped her adjust until she got on her feet.

"You wanted to see me, sir?" Ciena stepped inside, and the doors shushed closed.

"Have a seat, please." He gestured to one of the chairs and sat down on his own.

Ciena's mind started to race again, forcing away the short-lived peace from a moment ago. She couldn't help thinking about every interaction she had had with guests over the last week or two, every job she had done and every conversation with station employees as she took the short walk across the room to the chair. What could this be about?

Commander Hamelin lifted a tablet and turned it to face her. "So, I see you're leaving us. I got your application to end your station contract a few days ago."

She relaxed in her seat. So this was why he'd called her in. "Yes, sir. I turned my papers in a little early because I wanted to give you time to find someone to apprentice under me before I left."

"I do appreciate that. And I've already found a strong candidate for the position. He'll be on his way from Lutus and will arrive within a couple of weeks, once we settle everything." He cleared his throat and sat back in his chair. "There is another matter to discuss." He tapped the tablet a few times. "I called you in here today so that we could complete the exit paperwork, and begin the process of settling your accounts."

She folded her arms, gripping her elbows, sensing there was more to this meeting than simple paperwork she could do on her own.

"It seems you still owe the station about fifteen thousand clicks from your hospital stay. There were also fees associated with the expense of outfitting your business, along with the station tax."

The color drained from Ciena's face. Fifteen thousand clicks. It would take almost a year to save up that much. She could picture Abby's disappointed face in her mind when she broke the news.

"Sir...this can't be right. I was told by the head nurse herself that I didn't need to worry about my stay in the hospital once I began working here. Every supply I've ever used or piece of equipment I've borrowed was for work on the station or its guests." She glared at him, daring him to contradict her.

"That's all true if you are a station employee. You are not. You never signed on as an official part of our staff, which is why you are free to leave now, if you choose. You are a freelance contractor. If, after five years, you had still been working with us and in good standing with the station, those fines would be absorbed and you would no longer owe them." He looked chagrined. "She misspoke. I'm sorry, you weren't informed properly."

"Are you kidding me?" Ciena spat. "I've worked hard here. I pay my rent on time and my contractor tax without complaint. I don't even know what this *station tax* is." She stood, looking down at the commander. "I can't stay here for another year! I need to get to Abby. You remember her, right? My little sister, the one *you* sent to live in an orphanage while I was unconscious in your hospital wing." She swallowed hard against her tightening throat. "You sent her away, without my permission, without anyone's permission, and I've been trying to get back to her ever since!"

Commander Hamelin held up his hand to stop her rant. "Ciena, enough. First of all, ignorance of certain protocols is not reason enough to invalidate them. We can't have people coming to our station, feeding on our hospitality, and skipping out the first chance they get. It's not a sustainable business model. And this station is a business, like it or not. Second of all, I sent your sister away to a place that is meant for children. She had no family--"

"She had me!" Ciena yelled, interrupting him.

"Yes, and we didn't expect you to actually survive." The commander paused, looking awkward. "I'm sorry, but it's true. It may not have been the best decision, but we did what we thought was right at the time. Ships heading that way don't come by very often. If we didn't send her then, she may have been waiting for six months or more."

"Every piece of material I have ever used has gone to benefit the station." She pulled the siren's pipe out of her pocket and held it up. "This pipe is my invention. Mine. Without it, you wouldn't be getting nearly as many ships passing through this station as you do, and you know it! There is no reason for you to charge me more."

Commander Hamelin put up his hands, "Ciena, calm down. That is something else I needed to discuss with you." His fatherly tone made her even more angry.

Ciena backed away, knocking the chair over. How could he do this to her?

She was being held hostage. They needed her.

She narrowed her eyes and gritted her teeth, glaring at the

commander. "*Sir*. I have a schedule to keep." She gave him a curt nod, then spun on her heel and stalked out of the room.

Commander Hamelin called after her, "Ciena, wait. I wasn't finished. I wanted to talk to you about your pipe and—"

A mumbled voice over Commander Hamelin's intercom interrupted him and he didn't follow after her.

CHAPTER 3

PEOPLE BUSTLED about the shuttle bay, loading items into the open cargo doors of the mining ship. Along one wall of the room, two men and a woman chatted while buttoning up their suits and fastening gear into place.

Ciena marched up to Kienn and pushed him.

His feet scuffled, and he rolled against the wall, trying to keep his balance.

"You knew! You knew what was going on. Did you help plan it too? You're supposed to be my friend!" All activity in the bay stopped. Everyone stared at them.

"What's going on?" Kienn looked around at the spectators. "Look, we can talk about this later. I swear, I didn't--"

"You don't need to explain. It's perfectly clear that you and your father are just holding me hostage. No one else matters. Not me, and certainly not a 7-year-old little girl who's been isolated from the only family she has left for over two years while slowly working herself to death in a labor camp masquerading as an orphanage!" Hot tears spilled over the edges of her wide, maddened eyes. She couldn't hold them back any longer.

He grabbed her elbow and led her away from the others.

"Look. I really have to go. But I think there's been a misunder-standing or something. I'll talk to you about it tonight."

"No. There's nothing to talk about." She pulled her arm out of his grip.

"Kienn," a middle-aged woman called out from the open loading platform on the shuttle. "We need to leave."

"I'll find you when I get back," he said, shaking his head as he turned and headed for the shuttle.

Ciena ran in the opposite direction, out the doors and down the corridor, drawing stares along the way. Her vision was too blurred to see the faces of those she passed, and she was glad for that.

It hurt to breathe. Her lungs felt like they were filled with stones, grating against each other and weighing her down. After several minutes, she stopped running. Her shoulders ached and her head throbbed.

Ciena wrapped her arms around her stomach trying to lessen the feeling of nausea working its way into her chest. Had she been too harsh with Kienn? No. No, this *was* a big deal. For over two years she had been meticulously counting every click, calculating how much money it would take to get to Abby, move them both to a new planet, and find a place to call home. Now, she had to break the news to her sister that she wasn't coming, and she didn't know how much longer it'd be.

The com-link clipped to her belt buzzed, alerting her that the ship scheduled to dock this afternoon was on its way to the designated bay. She drew in a deep breath and her jaw trembled as she exhaled. *Time to suck it up. If you ever want to get off this floating prison, you've got to get to work.*

Ciena's trap was over half full, but she was already running behind. She didn't want to take the time to dismantle the RATs and empty it out. There would be plenty of time for that later since she no longer had any plans. She frowned at the anger starting to rise.

Her father would have never stood for this ridiculous five-year protocol. Then again, he wouldn't have taken so long to rescue Abby. He would have figured something else out. She was failing him and her mother, failing them all.

Before she realized it, she was standing in front of the open cargo door to a large freighter ship. The crew had been allowed to disembark earlier in the day, but the ship itself had only been allowed to dock for decontamination an hour earlier.

Grateful for the already open door, Ciena headed in and got to work. Standing in the middle of the cargo bay, she plugged her pipe into the slot on the side of the Faraday trap and flipped the switch on. An erratically blinking green light on the side indicated it was sending out the subtle pulses and signals that called the RATs in.

Within minutes, several RATs scurried out of the ship towards her. She picked them up one by one and tossed them into the trap. Once they were all collected, she hit the EMP button and shut them down.

The next step always took the longest and Ciena hated the cramped spaces almost as much as she hated being tethered to a space suit outside the station, but, for once, she welcomed the quiet seclusion of the maintenance tubes. She opened a large side panel on the inside wall of the cargo bay and pushed the trap through the opening in front of her, then climbed in after it.

She lifted and fit the panel door in place behind her, as she always did to keep anyone from tripping over it, then pulled out her pipe to begin scanning for RATs. As she tuned the dial, she heard footfalls on the landing bay floor coming toward the ship.

She turned the handle on the panel, hoping to give them a heads-up that she'd be working in the tubes, but before she pushed it open a familiar voice made her stop dead. Her hair stood on end. She knew him. She would never forget that voice.

"…you sure they're down? No chance for outgoing communications at all?" The voice was low and faintly accented. A chill crept up Ciena's spine. It was definitely him. It was Captain Lars.

Shouts erupted in her mind and memories came to life. Her father fighting a man. Yelling to get to the pods. A chair smashing down again and again on his attacker. *Katha. Katha. Katha.* That horrid curse. The flash of light. A body on the floor. Her mother's screams, then silence as the pod launched.

Ciena's chest and throat ached all over again as she forced the memories back. Those men, those pirates, were now on this space station. She cupped her hands over her mouth and sucked air through her fingers, in and out, letting the warm breath bathe her face with each exhale.

"Yes, sir. Cye finished reprogramming them over a quarter-hour ago. They have no idea outgoing messages are blocked, and we've successfully diverted all inbound ships scheduled to dock for the next twenty-four hours." His accent was so thick, it was hard to make out what he was saying.

The limping man that had cursed in the common room earlier had been on the crew. *I never interacted with him though. I couldn't be sure, before. I still should have said something. How could I have forgotten? Stupid, stupid, stupid.*

"Our men are in position as well?"

"Just waiting on your order, sir."

Ciena wrapped her arms around her knees to keep herself from shaking, nudging the panel with her elbow as she adjusted. The panel handle shifted, and clicked softly as it settled itself into place.

"What was that?"

"What was what?"

Ciena froze. Afraid to move. Afraid to breathe.

"I thought I heard something." The men stopped talking.

Ciena's heartbeat thrummed in her ears with such force she worried they could hear it through the silence.

"Nevermind," the man who wasn't Captain Lars said.

"Don't get all jumpy on me now. It was likely the ship settling," Captain Lars said, scolding the other man. "Let's do this before someone gets *wise*," he growled the last word as if that would be a real irritation to deal with.

The familiar static blip of an old-fashioned radio communicator powering on filled the silent room. "It's a go. Take out the commander, now. Let's move."

CHAPTER 4

THE STATION'S sirens blared to life. Someone inside had sounded the alarm. Someone was fighting back.

Ciena found it hard to think while adrenaline bounced around inside her skull. Could the station guards stop them? What type of protocols would the station follow? Would she end up as collateral damage as they opened fire on the retreating ship?

She shuffled backward, careful to make as little noise as possible, not trusting the sirens to completely muffle her movement. The vent a few feet back would have a view of the bay. She pushed a vent blade, and it tilted open.

Three men stood at the bottom of the ramp leading into the ship. Their guns were trained on the docking bay's exit doors, and their fingers rested on the triggers.

Her mind raced, trying to think of something to draw the guards' attention away. Except that would never work. With three of them, and how far she'd have to run to reach the doors, there was no way she could hope to escape, even with the perfect distraction.

There had to be something else.

If she could stall them for a few minutes; it might give the station guards time to intervene. This ship was similar to the one she'd been on years ago with her family. She should be able to get to the controls of the ship and cause a malfunction that prevented it from disembarking.

Too late. Subtle vibrations moved through the tube accompanied by a barely audible thrum. The ship's engines had turned on.

The guards moved to the exit doors and pointed their guns down the hall. Ten new pirates filed into the bay carrying loot from the station, and each wore a gas mask of some kind.

Shouts and the sound of large objects being heaved on board and dropped with deep, hollow thumps loud enough to be heard over the sirens and the ship's engines.

Two of the pirates near the back carried a large cube with pulsing blue lights. A second dark cube followed. Ciena's heart skipped a beat.

They had the energy modulator that helped the station regulate and redistribute the power it captured from the distant sun. Without it, the station would run out of power in its backup cells within a few days. They had the main cube, and the backup. The occupants of the station would freeze to death as the environmental shield failed and temperature systems could no longer keep up with the demands of the station.

They have no idea outgoing messages are blocked.

They couldn't even call for help. Contact from this far out wasn't regular, and any radio silence that lasted less than a day would likely be discounted as solar interference of some kind.

The lack of exchanged fighting and the steady, but not rushed manner of the pirates made Ciena's blood run cold. Was everyone already dead?

Ciena set her jaw. *No. I will not watch this happen and do nothing. Not again.* Thinking furiously, she counted the few assets she had. Her pipe, her trap, items left in the tube's maintenance stations, access to a limited number of ship systems–thanks to her station engineer pass, if they hadn't deactivated it–and her brain.

She let the buzzing adrenaline in her head spin, conjuring up scenarios along with their probabilities of success, until she landed on the only one that had any chance of succeeding. She needed to use the RATs to disable the ship, grab the energy modulator cubes and escape inside an evacuation pod. That might give other travelers a chance to come to the station, find out what had happened and call the Galactic Alliance to hunt down the pirates. And find her. Maybe. It was a plan. A stupid, suicidal plan, but it was better than doing nothing.

———

The ship shuddered and the bay doors slammed closed with an ominous clank. The loading area was crowded with crates, bags, and armloads of goods pillaged from the station. Men and women alike removed facemasks, clapped each other on the back and laughed.

"Hold off on your celebrations. We're not out of the woods, yet. We've still got to make it through the sling before we're home safe," said the bearded man she'd seen earlier with Kienn. He limped after Captain Lars, heading to the prow of the ship, and waved for the others to follow.

Using the sling was the only reason she could figure that they would have blocked outgoing communications, so that made sense. If the station was able to get word out about their attack, all of the hyper-jump slings would be frozen until the Galactic Federation released them.

It would be a little over thirty minutes before the band of pirates made it to the hyperjump point. Ciena pulled the cylindrical pipe out of her pocket. She held it to her chest, and closed her eyes, saying a silent prayer to the energy of the universe and any god out there who might be listening. Before she opened her eyes, a picture of the full and vibrant common room filled her mind. She could almost hear the carefree laughter from only a few hours ago. This plan of hers was their only chance. She was their only hope.

"Let's move," she whispered, defiantly mocking the words one of the pirates had used mere moments ago. She crawled along the twisted maintenance tunnels that crisscrossed around the ship like some sort of unseen cage, pushing the RAT trap in front of her. It was lucky that she'd spent the last two years crawling around in every imaginable kind of ship and that most were built intuitively similar to help maintenance crews, otherwise she'd definitely end up lost in this maze.

Ten exhausting minutes later, she found herself beneath the engine room. A locked panel door blocked her way. Red lights on the code-box blinked in time with the pulse jumping in her neck. She hesitated. If her access code had been deleted, attempting to unlock this door would initiate a ship wide alert. There was no time for debate. It would either work, or it wouldn't. She bit her lip, flipped open the code-box, and scanned her wrist. For a gut wrenching second, nothing happened. Then, the lights turned green and the panel door slid open. *I'm going to die of a heart attack before the pirates ever find me,* she thought, looking up at the now exposed massive circuit box and its dancing display of lights.

Wasting no time, she slid open the drawer that held spare fuses and pocketed the few left there, then pulled more fuses from auxiliary and back-up systems that she hoped wouldn't be noticed.

Once she had enough fuses to repair the rats in her trap, she brought the pipe out of her pocket, flipped up the top, and popped the housing off the tuning dials. She gently pulled some of the wires free and stripped off the plastic insulation, then set to work, connecting those wires to others in the circuit box.

After making calculations in her head, she turned the dials on the pipe, tapped out a beat, and held her breath. A little green light on the side of the pipe began flashing, indicating that it was transmitting the signal over all of the ship's outgoing channels. Even at max output, the signal was subtle enough that it would be dismissed as static and simply filtered out if anyone decided to use the comms. Hopefully. But any RAT within one hundred hectares should be frantically making their way to the ship, following the siren's song from her pipe.

The pipe itself dangled from the circuit box. Its weight threatened to dislodge the wires from their housings. Ciena reached up and unthreaded one of the ribbons from her hair. The sight of the purple satin strand made her chest tighten. She had to make it out of here. For Abby.

With a renewed sense of haste, she used the ribbon to tie the pipe securely to a thick cable inside the circuit box. *I'll buy you a whole slew of purple ribbons, Abby...if I somehow survive this.* She tugged on the pipe to make sure it would hold, then pressed the button that closed the panel door.

Now for part two of the plan. She needed to get the RAT trap as far away from here as possible before she replaced their fuses and unleashed them. It was too risky to let them loose so close to the pipe. It needed time to do its job.

Ciena wrapped her jacket around the trap to muffle the noise as she pushed it so she could move faster than before.

This worked better than she'd hoped, until the heavy box caught against a raised rivet. It ripped her jacket and drummed against the bottom of the box as her momentum carried it forward. The sound reverberated down the corridor.

"Hey, what was that?" a muffled voice said.

"I dunno. Sounded like it came from over here."

Ciena's chest felt like it held a couple of caged bats, fluttering and banging into each other as they tried to escape. She lifted the lid to the trap and grabbed a RAT. A rush of heat ran through her body, and she nearly dropped the little robot twice as her shaking hands struggled to replace the fried fuse and turn the blasted thing on. She tossed it back down the corridor and pulled the box behind her around a bend in the tube.

"It's coming from in there. Get that panel off, Cye."

The noise of the panel clicking open so close to where she sat, combined with trying not to breathe so hard after all the physical exertion, made sweat at the crown of her head bead up and trickle down her face. It itched as it dripped over the tip of her nose. She resisted the urge to wipe it away, hugging her knees even tighter.

"Bah! It's just a stupid RAT." Several flashes of light from a photon gun illuminated the tube.

With each one, Ciena squeezed tighter and tried not to jump.

A flashlight scanned the walls, casting odd shadows through tendrils of smoke wafting off what was left of the RAT. "I thought that exterminator was supposed to get rid of all of 'em. Didn't that station have that prodigy kid? Looks like it was all a load of solar wind."

"They're bound to miss one once in a while, Jeb. 'Sides, it ain't right to talk ill of the soon-to-be-dead," he said in a mockingly pious voice.

"Yeah, we exterminated their exterminator."

They both chuckled.

The acrid smell of melted metal drifted over Ciena, and she swallowed down a cough trying to claw its way out of her throat. Her eyes watered with the effort of holding it back. They needed to leave. Now.

The panel made a *whump, whump, click* sound as they fit it back in place. Their voices faded until the only sounds were the thrum of the ship's engine and the blood pulsing in Ciena's ears. Once she was sure they were gone, she buried her face in her elbow to muffle the sound, and coughed hard to clear her throat.

She didn't trust herself to push the box any farther. She'd have to set the RATs loose here and hope that they were far enough away from her pipe not to reach it for a while. She needed the signal going strong for as long as possible. One by one, she pulled the little robots out of the trap and fitted them with new fuses—grateful that the maintenance stations in the tubes had been well stocked—while at the same time adjusting some of their circuitry and programming. A normal Autonomous Trasher, even a rogue one, would spend weeks searching for components to repair itself, or salvage, before tearing apart the "junk" it came across. She bypassed that particular protocol on each of the RATs as she pulled them out, setting them into a destructive frenzy.

They squirmed and wriggled in her hand, eager to set to work. Multiple plier-like claws reached for objects before she even set them down. Compartments in the RATs opened up with lasers and clamps, setting to work on the pipes and frame.

The RATs soundlessly cut down and tore away pieces of pipe, wires and walls, working their way out in the direction of the hull. Ciena couldn't help smiling. These were incredible machines. Incredibly terrifying. Most people didn't realize how quiet RATs actually were, nor what they were capable of. Detecting them was rather difficult, and they could do a lot of damage before they were discovered, which is what made her job on the station so valuable.

Ciena left the RATs to do their dirty work and crawled back toward the loading bay. The ship slowed unnaturally fast before she reached the bay, causing her stomach to lurch. There wouldn't be a noticeable change inside the ship as it decelerated unless the gravitational dampeners were damaged.

Hopefully, that meant that the other RATs in the quadrant were responding to her signal, or maybe the RATs inside the ship were doing more damage than she had anticipated. Either way, she didn't have much time to carry out the rest of her plan.

Her knees hurt from knocking against the tunnel floors. She'd have bruises tomorrow for sure, but she pushed through the pain until she saw a familiar vent above the loading bay.

Once she reached it, she peeked through the slits. Objects plundered by the pirates littered the floor, including the two energy modulator cubes in the middle of the room. The guards were long gone and all was quiet.

The panel door made a popping noise as she pushed it open. Her shoulders stiffened and her ears rang as she strained to hear any movement. Nothing but the silent breathing of the ship drifted back to her.

She waited a handful of seconds, just to be sure, then carefully dropped to the floor. As soon as her feet touched the ground, her skin came to life, hair standing on end, seeming to sense the very air around her.

Before she lost her nerve, she sped to the middle of the room and hid behind a crate. Step by step, she made her way to the Cube and laid a shaking hand on it, relieved they hadn't dismantled it for its valuable parts yet. She wrapped her arms around one of the cubes and bent backwards to lift it off the ground. It was a lot heavier than it looked. She couldn't just tuck it under her arm and carry it off to an evac pod, much less two of them.

Looking around at the crowded room of stolen loot, Ciena saw what she needed. Leaning against one of the crates was an airball hover-pad. She retrieved it and carefully pushed the energy modulators onto the pad, stacking one on top of the other. A musical power-up tone sounded when she turned on the hover-pad, and she jumped back, cursing.

Her heart raced madly as she pushed the cubes toward the doorway. It was working. They glided easily with the help of the hover-pad.

The door out of the cargo bay loomed in front of her. This final barrier to freedom also separated her from men who would kill her first and not bother to ask questions later. She couldn't leave the room completely unarmed. No guns, poles or any other obvious weapons lay among the stolen goods. Everything she could see was too big, too soft or too awkward to wield.

A shiny red tool locker a few feet away caught her eye. Inside the door on a hook hung a large heavy wrench. She seized it and slung it over her shoulder.

Steeling herself to run the gauntlet, she took a deep breath and punched the button to open the doors. They hissed open smoothly, and she started to push the hover pad over the threshold. Without warning it jolted to a stop, and powered down.

Now was not the time for stupid malfunctions. Looked like she owed Kienn an apology, too. She muted the power-up button before resetting it and turning it back on. The second it lifted off the floor she shoved it out the door.

No sooner had her foot stepped into the hallway than a shrill alarm burst the silence. The sound hit her body like a jolt of electricity and every muscle tightened in response. The urge to run and hide took hold. She used the cubes on the hover-pad as a shield, and sprinted down the corridor.

A loud, harsh voice barked over the ship's intercom system, "All men to stations. Emergency procedure delta in place."

Ciena relaxed a fraction. She hadn't activated an alarm. This was a general alert, and she hoped she knew why.

She turned a corner and saw her prize. Midway down the hall a row of escape capsules with clear reinforced glass doors lined the wall. She had made it. With the help of the wrench and some effort, she pried the control panel off the wall next to the first capsule she came to. She studied the box for a few seconds, found the wire she wanted and pulled it free from its fitting. Then on an impulse, she pulled the wire that resealed the launch door, and shoved the panel roughly back into place.

As soon as she pushed the button to eject the pod, an alert would sound and the whole ship would be notified that an evacuation pod had been activated. It took thirty seconds for the pod to pressurize. She didn't have any idea how to disable the ship's weapons system. Maybe if she had more time she could figure it out. But she didn't. After she ejected, she'd be a sitting duck. Like her mom had been.

Last time she was in an evacuation pod, a malfunction had nearly killed her. Gritting her teeth, she lifted a trembling hand and pushed the button that opened the pod door. Once the cubes were in, there was very little room left for her, but she squeezed in beside them and shut the door.

Ciena stretched across the cubes until her finger tips slid under the release handle. She pulled hard, but the handle didn't release, making her slam her elbow into the wall behind her. The way the cubes sat wedged against the handle made it impossible to pull down. No matter what angle she tried, she couldn't make it work.

Her heart raced, knowing she was wasting precious seconds. She had to try something else. She maneuvered herself into the small space on the side of the pod and forced the cubes toward the front, moving them away from the release handle.

She almost had it when a large, broad shouldered man with thick brows over dark deep-set eyes came around the corner followed by several others. It was him. Captain Lars.

She willed herself to turn invisible, hoping they wouldn't see her, hoping they'd keep walking. Men climbed into the other evacuation pods, ignoring her. She thought for a moment it'd worked, until Captain Lars stopped right in front of her.

He tried to open the pod door, but the keypad wouldn't respond.

The override wouldn't work, if the wires were pulled. Her foresight had paid off. He slammed a fist into the pad in frustration after several attempts.

Ciena braced her feet against the pod wall and pushed against the cubes, moving them just far enough away to free the handle. As soon as she knew it was clear, she gripped the release handle and pulled.

A mechanical voice filled the pod. "Prepare for departure. Pod will launch in thirty seconds. Thirty, twenty-nine, twenty-eight…"

The captain's head snapped up. His face went from surprised and confused to raging anger as he spotted the cubes and the stowaway behind them. "Open this door!" His words were barely audible after passing through the thick pane of synthetic glass.

She stared back at him, not answering, not moving.

He roared and slammed his massive fist against the door, shaking the entire pod, "Open up!"

He took several steps back, and from his posture, Ciena could tell he intended to run at the pod, but his foot caught on something. The wrench! He picked it up and lifted it above his head with a wicked grin and slammed it down on the pod, over and over again.

Thwack!

Thwack!

Thwack!

Ciena flinched with every strike.

The commander screamed and his eyes bulged.

"…nine, eight, seven, six…" the voice continued calmly.

The wrench connected more solidly as Lars raged.

Thwack!

Thwack!

He was going to break through.

With a sudden jolt, the pod exploded out of the ship and Ciena was thrown against the cubes as she hurtled away from Lars.

The captain grabbed madly at the side of the ship. It did no good. Strong as he was, he was no match for the relentless vacuum of space. He flailed as he was sucked into the inky blackness.

Ciena's stomach turned. Knowing what would happen when she disabled the airlock on the evacuation pods and seeing the result were two different things. She wanted to believe she had to do it, that it was simply one more failsafe to ensure they didn't get away, but the part of her that lived in the nightmare he and his crew created knew it was more than that. Maybe now she could finally move on.

She watched the tumbling figure grow smaller and smaller, as she continued to drift farther and farther away.

A dark gray cloud enveloped the ship and it took her a moment to realize that couldn't be what was happening. She focused on the mass, and her eyes widened in shock. The 'cloud' was made up of thousands of tiny mechanical beasts. The ship looked like an abandoned piece of bread at a picnic, covered in a writhing mass of ants. She didn't know there were this many RATs in the entire quadrant. How had they gotten here so fast? She stared in disbelief. It had worked.

A few more pods ejected from the other side of the ship. The few surviving pirates had packaged themselves up neatly for the Galactic Federation to collect when they arrived. The pods had no steering capabilities or propulsion, other than the initial burst, meaning they were all now at the mercy of whoever came to their rescue.

Rescue. How long would it be before she would get out of here? Sabotage and escape was all she had room for in her mind after she made her plans back in the tube.

A flat mechanical voice cut off her train of thought.

"Pressurization failure imminent, approximately one hour to full failure. Rescue beacon has been activated."

CHAPTER 5

NOT AGAIN. Not another failure.

Ciena tried to breathe, but couldn't get her lungs to pull in any air. She teetered on the edge of complete hyperventilation. She focused on her feet, wiggling her toes one by one and breathed out as hard as she could, which disrupted her mind enough to calm her down and allow her lungs to work again.

Freaking out wouldn't help anything, but she'd been here before. She knew exactly how it felt to slowly run out of air and warmth, wondering which system would fail first while trying to avoid looking out at the floating debris and what should have been the other survivors. She had strapped the only backup oxygen mask in the pod to Abby after she fell asleep at her feet and passed out herself only minutes later. That was over two years ago, but waking up in the Hespres II space station hospital wing, cold to her bones, unable to get warm or breathe on her own was a memory so vivid that it would always feel like yesterday.

She couldn't give up. She wasn't a child anymore. There had to be something she could do. It couldn't end like this.

She wished she hadn't yelled at Kienn.

He had always been such a good friend and—and he wasn't on the station!

The cubes were annoyingly in the way as she tried to shimmy past them to reach the communications panel. She unclipped the comm device from her belt and fitted it into the port. She prayed that the signal on the pod would be strong enough to reach him. "Kienn? Kienn, it's Ciena. Can you hear me?"

Silence.

She waited a few seconds and tried again. "Kienn, it's Ciena. Please." Soft static was the only response.

She closed her eyes and cold tears streaked down her hot face. "Kienn, please. Are you there?"

Nothing.

She turned and stared out the transparent door. Several bodies floated in the space surrounding what was left of the ship. Her stomach clenched, in spite of herself. These people were the reason her parents were gone. The reason Abby was so far away from her. The reason they never reached their new home. They didn't deserve her sympathy.

"Oh, Abby, I'm sorry I have to leave you like this." She leaned against the cubes and groaned. Her head felt heavy and all she wanted to do was sleep. Was the pod failing already? She was so tired. If the station didn't get the cubes back, they would all die too. This was a disaster. Maybe Kienn would find the cubes in time, even if she didn't make it.

The pod speakers crackled, and a green light above the comm turned on. "I thought you didn't want to talk to me?"

Ciena jumped and smacked her fist against the controls in her rush to hit the outgoing com key.

"Kienn? Where are you?" Relief poured over her like a bucket of water and she fought back the urge to break down in sobs.

"We're just finishing up here. We found a big pocket of water, so we stayed longer than we planned mapping it out. We'll be heading back to the station in just a few. You decide you want to hear–"

"Listen, Kienn. While you were away from the station, we were attacked. The comms were knocked out."

There was a brief silence. "How are *you* contacting me then?"

"I'm stuck in an evacuation pod by the sling point. I...I destroyed the attacker's ship, but my pod is losing pressure. I have less than an hour before it shuts down. Even if you can't make it here in an hour, you have to get to the pod. I have both of the station's energy modulation cubes with me."

"What? The energy modulation cubes?"

"Yeah, I'll explain more later. Can you please just hurry? I really don't want to spend three weeks in that hospital again."

"Are you hurt? I mean, did they do anything to you?" She could hear the anxious concern in his voice and was glad to know he still cared, despite her emotional outburst earlier.

"My pipe and trap are gone, which hurts, I guess. But physically, I'm fine."

"Good." He seemed relieved. "Is there anyone else with you?"

"No, it's just me and the cubes."

"Okay, give me a second." The comm went silent, but the light above it stayed a steady green, showing the channel was still open. He'd likely stepped away to inform his team what was going on.

After what felt like far too long for such a simple conversation, the comm crackled and Kienn's voice replaced the silence in the pod. "Ciena, hang on. We're on our way."

"Kienn, wait." She thought about mentioning what the pirates had said about his father, but she couldn't bring herself to tell him. He'd find out on his own soon enough.

"What?" he prodded.

"The attackers wore gas masks when they left the station, so be careful when you go back there. And," she swallowed against the lump in her throat—"and, I'm sorry about earlier. I wanted you to know, just in case–"

"Stop. I'm not listening to any just-in-cases. Just hang on. I'll be there soon. I promise."

———

Ciena sat up, feeling dizzy and nauseated. For the second time in her life she woke up in the hospital wing at the space station. Her body ached in an all too familiar way, and it felt like her bones had been replaced with ice.

"Good to see you're awake."

Ciena turned to see Commander Hamelin a few beds down from her, hooked to several machines, shooing away a nurse who had been taking his vitals.

"Commander, I thought that you were…um, I heard the pirates say that they were going to take you out," Ciena said, pulling the blanket up to her chin and wrapping it around her shoulders. Despite her lingering anger, she was relieved to see he was alive.

"Yes, well. They did try. Thanks to some clever engineering on this station, and a lot of luck, I survived. I guess I'm tougher than they expected." He chuckled wryly, then grabbed his side with a grimace. He turned and called out to the nurse who had just walked away. "Jasmine, bring out another warm blanket, would you?"

The nurse nodded and left the room.

"Were there any casualties?" she asked, not wanting to know, but unable to get the question out of her head.

"Yes, three. Three too many. Two security guards from Engineering and a guest who tried to intervene." He shook his head. "Thankfully, they miscalculated the amount of poisonous gas they needed. Instead of being lethal, it acted as a potent sedative. Maybe that's what they intended, they didn't need us dead yet, just incapacitated. They knew they wouldn't be leaving any witnesses on the station once the backup batteries died."

The door to the hospital wing hissed open, and Kienn stepped inside the room. He stopped mid-stride, and his face split into a wide smile. "You're awake!"

Ciena smiled up at him. "You know me. I hate sleeping the day away almost as much as I hate being cold."

He laughed and rushed over to stand in the space between Ciena's bed and his father's.

Commander Hamelin took a warm blanket from the nurse who had just returned with it and tossed it to Ciena.

She hugged it to her chest, letting the warmth spread through her arms. "Thank you." It was hard to stay mad at Commander Hamelin when he kept doing nice things. But that didn't mean she was going to let everything go.

Kienn held out his hands as if he wanted to help her unfold the blanket and put it on properly.

Ciena smiled at him and gave him a resigned sigh while spreading the blanket out over her legs.

Commander Hamelin waved his hands, as though clearing the air of smoke and said, "Anyway, Ciena, we both wanted to talk to you, and it really can't wait." He passed a tablet to Kienn, who handed it to her. She took it hesitantly and scrolled to the bottom where a balance of negative forty thousand clicks was highlighted.

"Just so there isn't any confusion, the station is paying *you* twenty-five thousand clicks. It's slightly more than we were offering before, as some of the docked ships chipped in to cover your medical expenses both from now and from before, so those will all be cleared, and the plans for your pipe are obviously a little more valuable than we thought," Commander Hamelin said.

"Wait, what do you mean by *more* than before?" she asked.

"Well, apparently, Father didn't get a chance to negotiate

with you earlier. He did bring you in to settle your accounts and part of that was offering to buy your pipe from you. He thought it'd be best to get the bad stuff out of the way first, because his higher ups insist that he account for every click entrusted to this station. You never got past that part, though," Kienn said, giving her a *don't you feel foolish* grin.

"But that wasn't. . . I could have sworn…" she stammered. Her face heated up and she dropped her head into her hands.

"I obviously hadn't managed to give you any of that information." Commander Hamelin gave her an apologetic smile, once again adopting that fatherly persona.

"I don't know what to say. I'm sorry." Ciena felt her face flush and wanted to crawl under the blankets to hide.

Kienn cleared his throat. "It's all in the past. We have something more important to take care of right now." He looked at his father for support, who nodded at him. "There's a transport ship scheduled to stop here on its way to Tritos. It will be making a stop at Ophelia, first. My aunt is traveling on that ship. We were hoping you would consider bringing Abby *here* to live with you, on the Hespres II?" He paused and looked at her.

Ciena couldn't be sure she heard him right. What if this was another misunderstanding?

When she didn't say anything Kienn rushed on. "We can book her passage today and start the paperwork with the orphanage. My aunt can act as her guardian until she arrives. You know, since she isn't twelve yet, and can't travel alone. The money you've saved can pay for her passage here, instead of your passage there. Of course, we wouldn't be buying your pipe any longer if you stayed. So, we'd have to reconfigure all of those numbers. It's up to you. No pressure."

Ciena looked up at the ceiling, shook her head and laughed as tears slid down her cheeks. This was the only family she had left. This *was* her home.

"Well, I had been looking forward to punching Pedra in the nose when I collected Abby." Her body tingled, and goose bumps rose on her skin. "But, this is so much better. I would really, *really* like that."

"Me too," Kienn agreed.

"I can't wait to tell Abby," she said. "Oh! I've got to order some purple ribbon. Purple everything. We'll have a purple party. She'd love that, don't you think?" she asked Kienn.

"Absolutely." Kienn smiled broadly.

Ciena's heart swelled. She was really glad she wouldn't have to say goodbye to her best friend. "By the way," she said, "I think the station needs to invest in new hover-pads. The one I used to haul the cubes had some issues."

Kienn shoved her shoulder playfully. "See, I told you I wasn't making it up. Mine really did malfunction during our last match."

Commander Hamelin cut in before Ciena could reply, "We've already got some ordered. We were able to recover a lot of the stolen items, but not everything."

Kienn clapped his hands together and rubbed them in mock eagerness. "Great. Once the replacement equipment arrives, we'll have a proper rematch."

"Deal. I'll still beat you. In fact, I'll take on you and Abby both when she gets here, and I'll still win."

"You've sure got a lot of confidence for someone sitting in a hospital bed hooked up to machines," he said, giving her IV tube a playful flick.

Ciena folded her arms and gave what she hoped was an exaggeratedly smug look. "No, I've got the exact right amount of confidence after taking down a band of pirates on my own and getting my sister back all in the same day. Luck is definitely on my side. Not that I need it."

Kienn laughed and pulled her into a hug, resting his chin on the top of her head. "I'm really glad you're staying."

She still could hardly believe that Abby would be here in only a handful of weeks. A sudden realization jolted through her, and she pushed away from Kienn, looking up at him with wide eyes. "I need to get an official registered address so Abby can attend school here. I'm going to have to move out of guest quarters and get a real apartment." She paused, speaking the last part slowly. "We'll have a real address on the station. A real home."

Kienn pulled her back into his arms and squeezed tight. "Yes. Yes, you will. Welcome home, Ciena."

ABOUT THE AUTHOR

Deanna Young grew up in northwest New Mexico doing all the normal things a child of the desert does. She chased lizards and climbed cottonwood trees, built 'inventions' out of junkyard scraps, and grudgingly dealt with the ever-present New Mexican sand that seemed to take up permanent residence inside her shoes. It was amongst this gritty environment that Deanna discovered the value of stories. Whether spinning yarns for her siblings during the years they went without access to TV, or sitting on her father's lap while he read The Hobbit over and over until the cover wore thin, she learned that stories are about more than mere entertainment. Stories are about immersion, inspiration, and connection with others, both inside the pages and out. Love of the written word stayed with Deanna when she traded the majestic New Mexican mesas for the humble Oquirrh Mountains in northern Utah, where she currently resides with her family. Although she often misses the starry skies, dramatic sunsets, and mouth-watering green chili of her youth, she doesn't miss the omnipresent sand and heavy shoes. As a mother and/or caretaker to four kids, nine chickens, two cats, and a rambunctious dog she has plenty to keep her occupied. Thankfully, she still finds time to coax new creations out of her imagination and onto the page. Deanna's work can be found in several anthologies, including: Once Upon a Future Time Volume I and Volume II, A Fantasy Christmas—Tales From the Hearth, Something Lost, and Something Found. Deanna has also received accolades for her works including first place for the opening chapter of her nonfiction memoir Half Blue (yet to be published), and the Grand Prize for her flash fiction story The Scarf, which can be read at: https://www.saltandsagebooks.com/posts/2019/flash-fiction-grand-prize-winner/Flash Fiction GRAND PRIZE WINNER - Salt and Sage Books

Deanna's passion for storytelling, along with her writing skills continue to evolve and grow as she draws inspiration from her own life and the world around her. Follow her on Amazon, Facebook, and Instagram.